LITTLE SIMON

An imprint of Simon & Schuster Children's Publishing Division • 1230 Avenue of the Americas, New York, New York 10020 • First Little Simon hardcover edition April 2019 • Copyright © 2019 by Simon & Schuster, Inc. All rights reserved, including the right of reproduction in whole or in part in any form. LITTLE SIMON is a registered trademark of Simon & Schuster, Inc., and associated colophon is a trademark of Simon & Schuster, Inc. For information about special discounts for bulk purchases, please contact Simon & Schuster Special Sales at 1-866-506-1949 or business@simonandschuster.com. The Simon & Schuster Speakers Bureau can bring authors to your live event. For more information or to book an event contact the Simon & Schuster Speakers Bureau at 1-866-248-3049 or visit our website at www.simonspeakers.com.

Series designed by Laura Roode. The text of this book was set in Usherwood. Manufactured in the United States of America 0319 FFG   10 9 8 7 6 5 4 3 2 1 Cataloging-in-Publication Data is available for this title from the Library of Congress.

ISBN 978-1-5344-3301-4 (hc)
ISBN 978-1-5344-3300-7 (pbk)
ISBN 978-1-5344-3302-1 (eBook)

the adventures of
SOPHiE MOUSE

14

The Great Bake off

By Poppy Green • Illustrated by Jennifer A. Bell

LITTLE SIMON

New York London Toronto Sydney New Delhi

Contents

chapter 1

The Missing Ingredient

"Sophie," came a voice from downstairs. "Could you come down here?"

In her bedroom—which doubled as an art studio—Sophie set down her paintbrush right away. It was her mom calling, and she sounded worried.

Sophie knew her mother had a lot of baking to do that day. Lily Mouse's

bakery had gotten three big orders: a wedding cake, two dozen birthday cupcakes, and a batch of scones for the mayor's tea. And everything needed to be done by tomorrow! She'd brought her work home with her so she didn't have to spend day and night at the bakery.

Sophie scurried down the stairs. In the kitchen, her mom was frosting a layer of the wedding cake. Bowls, baking pans, and utensils crowded the countertop. Mrs. Mouse's apron was covered in flour. Her whiskers were drooping.

But she perked up when she saw Sophie.

"I sure could use an extra set of hands," she told Sophie. "I know you're busy working on a painting, but . . . would you mind?"

Mind? Sophie thought. She loved helping her mom bake. "What can I do?" Sophie asked. "Make the cupcakes? Glaze the scones? Decorate the cake?"

Mrs. Mouse smiled apologetically. "It's not that much fun," she explained. "I just realized I'm out of lemon extract. I need it for the scone glaze."

Oh no. Sophie felt an errand coming on.

"Would you run to Hattie's house?" Lily went on. "See if they have any? If they don't, I'm not sure what I'll do. I know I'm all out at the bakery!"

It wasn't really what Sophie felt like doing. But she wanted to help.

So Sophie went off down the path toward Hattie Frog's house. Hattie was one of Sophie's best friends— and closest neighbors. Hattie, her big sister, Lydie, and their parents lived on the bank of the stream.

What are the chances they have lemon extract? Sophie wondered. It was an unusual ingredient.

Halfway to Hattie's, Sophie's eyes fell on a patch of three-leaved plants.

"Wood sorrel!" she cried. "Yum!" She picked a few leaves. She nibbled as she walked on. Sophie had always loved its fresh, lemony flavor.

Sophie stopped again. She stared down at the leaves in her hand. Lemon! Could wood sorrel work in her mom's recipe?

Mrs. Mouse handed Sophie a mortar and pestle. Sophie put some wood sorrel into the bowl of the mortar. Then she used the pestle to grind it into a powder.

Meanwhile, Mrs. Mouse gathered the other ingredients. She measured and poured them into a mixing bowl.

Sophie backtracked to the patch of wood sorrel. She gathered as much as she could in her arms.

Then she hurried home to see what her mom would say.

9

— chapter 2 —

A Delicious Deal

Sophie watched her mom's face as she tasted the wood sorrel.

She took one bite. Then another. Then a third. And broke into a genuine smile.

"I never would have thought this," Mrs. Mouse said. "But try! Let's make the glaze with leaves and see what happen

Sophie added the ground wood sorrel. Lily whisked it all together.

"Time for a taste!" Lily said. She dipped two spoons into the glaze. She handed one to Sophie.

They tasted it at the same time. Mrs. Mouse beamed. "It's—"

"Really, really good!" Sophie cried.

Her mom took another taste. "Sweet. Lemony. Fresh and light," she said. "And I like the color!" The scone glaze was usually white. This version was a pretty pale green from the wood sorrel. "Green is perfect for the mayor's tea. I happen to know it's her favorite color!"

Mrs. Mouse pulled Sophie in for a hug. "Thank you, Sophie," she said. "You are a huge help."

Sophie's heart swelled with pride.

Mrs. Mouse went back to working on the wedding cake. Meanwhile, Sophie washed dishes and tidied up the counter. She picked up the recipe card for the glaze and put it back in her mom's recipe binder. As she did, a piece of paper fell out.

Tenth Annual
Firefly Springs Bake Off!

Bring your best baked treats.
Bring your baking skills.
Bring your creativity.
Come ready to think on your
feet, paws, and tails!

Sophie held the paper up. "Mom, are you going to enter this year?" she asked.

She had always wanted her mom to enter the bake off. It was a big baking contest held in a nearby village, and animals from all the surrounding villages came out to watch. The winner won the title of Year's Best Baker. Sophie just knew her mom could win!

But Sophie was also pretty sure
she knew the answer to her question.
Her mom never entered the contest—
usually because she was busy with
one thing or another.

Mrs. Mouse turned and saw the
paper. Suddenly her eyes twinkled

and her whiskers twitched. Sophie
knew that look. Her mom had an
idea.

"I will make you a deal,"
Mrs. Mouse said.
"I will enter
the bake
off . . . *if* you
agree to come
along and help
me."

Sophie jumped
up and down with
excitement. "It's
a deal!"

— chapter 3 —

Helpful Hints

Sophie woke up bright and early the next morning. She was going to help her mom deliver all the finished baked goods.

"I'll drop off the wedding cake this afternoon," Mrs. Mouse said. "And I'll take these cupcakes in to the bakery. The customer will be there to pick them up soon." Mrs. Mouse handed

Sophie the basket of scones. "When we get into town, do you think you could take these to the mayor?"

Sophie nodded, excited to handle the job on her own.

Together they walked along the path that led into the downtown of Pine Needle Grove. Then Lily went to the bakery while Sophie headed for

Town Hall. That was where Mayor Squirrel hosted Tea for the Town. It took place one Saturday a month. Citizens came to chat with the mayor. They asked questions or gave suggestions about improving the town.

Inside Town Hall, Mayor Squirrel
was putting out chairs. On a table
were several teapots and dozens of
teacups. And there were vases of
pretty wildflowers.

The mayor hurried over when she saw Sophie come in.

"How wonderful! The main attraction has arrived," Mayor Squirrel said with a chuckle. "I think some folks come just for your mom's treats."

Sophie presented the basket of scones. "I helped with the glaze," she said proudly.

The mayor peeked inside. "Th
look simply fantastic! And the gla
is green, my favorite color!" Mayo
Squirrel reached out to shake Sophie'
hand. "Well done, Sophie!"

Sophie beamed. Getting a com-
pliment from the mayor felt pretty
special.

"I'm going to help my mom next
week too!" Sophie blurted out. "She's
entering the bake off in Firefly
Springs!"

The mayor's eyes went wide.

"Well, well, well!" Mayor Squirrel
said. "Pine Needle Grovers in the

bake off! Why, we haven't had a contestant since . . . oh, it must be three years ago now! Mrs. Reeve, the librarian."

Mayor Squirrel shook Sophie's hand again. "Good luck to your mother, and good luck to you, Sophie Mouse! I know you will do a great job representing Pine Needle Grove."

Sophie said good-bye and headed for the bakery. But as she passed the library, she felt the urge to duck inside.

Sophie had questions for the librarian.

Mrs. Reeve was behind the check-out desk putting books on a rolling cart.

"Mrs. Reeve!" Sophie called out. In her excitement, she forgot where she was. Sophie covered her mouth, then continued in a whisper.

"My mom is entering the Firefly Springs Bake Off. And I'm going to help out! Mayor Squirrel said you entered a few years ago?"

Mrs. Reeve smiled. "Yes, indeed," she said. "Sadly, I did not win. But it was a wonderful and *interesting* experience."

She told Sophie about the different rounds of the contest. "The first round is pretty simple. Bakers bring a sampling of their best baked goods. The judges taste them and give each

baker a score. They say they like new, unusual flavor combinations. The more unique, the better. All this information is in the contest rules."

Sophie nodded. That sounded like useful advice.

"But the second round—phew!" Mrs. Reeve rubbed her brow as she remembered it. "It was a baking challenge. There was a lovely work-station with baking tools and a big brick oven. But the judges didn't tell us what the challenge was until the last minute. Then we had to decide what to make *and* bake it in one hour! It's a different challenge each year, so I have no idea what yours will be!"

Aha, thought Sophie. Suddenly a line from the flyer made more sense. *Come ready to think on your feet!*

Sophie thanked Mrs. Reeve for the advice.

"You're very welcome," the librarian replied. "Good luck! I will be rooting for you both."

— chapter 4 —

Flavor-ite Flavors

Sophie decided they needed to be better prepared. At the bakery, she asked her mom if she had read all the contest rules. Lily looked on the back of the bake off flyer.

"'First round,'" Lily read. "'Bakers may bring four types of baked goods for tasting and scoring by the judges.' It says they love unusual flavors."

Just like Mrs. Reeve said, thought Sophie.

"So we'll put our thinking caps on," Lily said. "Like we did for the Maple Festival. You had such great recipe ideas."

Sophie had so much fun helping her mom come up with new treats to sell at the festival. Orange and clove cakes. Poppy seed doughnuts. Cranberry-nut cookies. Lots of apple-maple combinations.

But this task seemed harder. They needed not just new recipes. They needed *new and unusual* flavor combinations.

"What does that mean exactly?" Sophie asked her mom.

Lily paused to think. "A combination that most folks wouldn't think of."

Sophie laughed.

"So things that *sound* like they'll taste bad together," she said, "but they actually taste good?"

"That's one way to look at it!" Mrs. Mouse said, also laughing.

This was going to be a challenge. It was time to start a list. Sophie pulled out her sketchbook and found a blank page. She wrote across the top:

Odd Flavor Combinations

Then Sophie started asking around.

On Monday, she told everyone at school about her mom entering the bake off.

"She's coming up with new recipes," Sophie said. "And I'm making a list of flavor combinations. What do you like that sounds weird but tastes great?"

Ben Rabbit opened his lunch box. "Here's one!" he said. He showed Sophie his sandwich. "Radish and jam!"

The other students wrinkled their noses—except for Ben's brother, James. "He's right!" James said. "It's good!" He took a big bite out of his own radish-and-jam sandwich.

Sophie wrote it down on her list.

Spicy + sweet
(like radishes and jam)

Hattie spoke up next. "I like sweet with salty," she said. "I put salt in my hot cocoa!"

Sophie made a note of it.

Sweet + salty
(like salted chocolate)

"Yum," said Sophie. "That does sound good."

After school, Sophie and her little brother, Winston, stopped at

the general store for a treat. Sophie
bought a peppermint. Winston went
for his usual—a giant gumball.

"Why do you get those every
time?" Sophie asked.

Winston popped the gumball into
his mouth. "It's two flavors in one!"
he cried. "The outside is super sour.
But the inside is super sweet!"

Sophie pulled out her list. *Sweet + sour (like Winston's gumball)*, she wrote.

All around town, folks had ideas.

"Coffee with cinnamon," said Mrs. Follet at Little Leaf Bookstore. "It's bitter but also spicy and sweet."

"Apples and peanut butter!" said Miss Olsen from the orchard.

"Potato chips on a sandwich," said Mr. Handy at Handy's Hardware. "Any kind of sandwich!"

By the end of the day, Sophie had a good list—and the town was abuzz with the news. Their very own Lily Mouse was going to be in the bake off!

— chapter 5 —

Recipes Gone Wrong

Every evening that week, Sophie and her mom tested out different recipes in their kitchen at home.

They had gathered a bunch of ingredients. Sophie had sorted them into flavor types.

For sweet, there was sugar, of course. But they also had honey, maple syrup, blueberries, strawberries,

raisins, and chocolate chips.

For sour, there were lemons, limes, cranberries, apple cider vinegar, crab apples, and more.

For spicy, they had all kinds of spices: cinnamon, cloves, cardamom, cayenne pepper, nutmeg, and ginger.

For bitter, there was coffee, baking cocoa, grapefruit, and root beer.

And for salty, they had salt and celery.

Sophie and her mom started with some of their favorite recipes. They tried adding one or two new ingredients to each one.

Mrs. Mouse put some lemon zest into her famous ginger snap recipe. Now they were lemon-ginger snaps.

"Spicy plus sweet plus sour," said Sophie.

Mrs. Mouse served them to Sophie's brother and dad. They were playing the role of judges.

"Mmm!" said Winston.

George Mouse nodded. "Different! I like it!"

They also liked Mrs. Mouse's raspberry chocolate torte. She had added a bit of cayenne pepper on top.

"Sweet and rich," said Mr. Mouse. "With a hint of spicy heat."

The carrot cake muffins were also a hit. Instead of vanilla frosting, Mrs. Mouse made them with coffee-cocoa frosting and cinnamon.

Sophie experimented too. She made a new version of her

mom's cheesecake: maple-cheddar cheesecake with a celery crust.

Winston only took one bite. He put his fork down without a word.

Mr. Mouse finished his piece. But Sophie could tell he didn't like it. *Oh well*, she thought. *Sometimes experiments don't work out.*

chapter 6

Next Sophie tried a twist on her mom's scallion and cheddar biscuits. "Everything is better with chocolate chips," said Sophie. "Right?"

Wrong. The flavors just clashed.

Luckily, her mom was having more success.

Cranberry-honey tarts? "Zingy!" Winston said.

Root beer–molasses mousse? "Wow!" Mr. Mouse said.

Poached crab apples in cardamom syrup? "Yum!" both of the judges said.

Sophie's mom was on a roll! She had a growing list of great new recipes. It would be hard to choose which items to bring to the bake off.

Sophie knew this was a good problem to have. And she was happy for her mom. But she was also disappointed.

Maybe Sophie's mom didn't need her help, after all.

A Parade of Sweets

Finally, it was Saturday. It was the day of the Tenth Annual Firefly Springs Bake Off!

Lily packed up right after breakfast. She filled two big baskets with the baked goods for round one.

"Raspberry chocolate tortes, check!" Lily said. "Cranberry-honey tarts, check! And carrot cake muffins

with coffee-cocoa frosting."

All three were new recipes that Lily had come up with. What would her fourth choice be?

"And let's bring the scones with wood sorrel glaze!" Lily said with a wink.

Sophie gasped with delight. Her mom was bringing one of her recipes! The scone recipe wasn't new. But the glaze was unique. Sophie hoped the judges would think so too.

The bake off started at ten a.m.
Firefly Springs was a half-hour
walk—at least! So by nine a.m., Lily
and Sophie were ready to go. But
Winston hadn't finished his cereal.

Mr. Mouse shooed them out the
door. "You two get started," he said.

"Winston and I will follow in a few minutes. I know the way."

So off they went. Lily carried one basket and Sophie carried the other. Sophie's basket was heavier than she expected. She held on tight, determined not to drop it.

They took the path into Pine Needle Grove. They would go through the center of town, into the forest on the other side, and on to Firefly Springs.

Sophie and Lily had only gone a few hundred paces when they heard the snap of a twig behind them. Then there were running footsteps, getting louder and louder.

Sophie turned.

Hattie was running after them. "Wait up!" she called. "Can we walk with you?"

Lydie was right behind her. "I've never been to a bake off!" she said. "I'm so excited to come watch and cheer you on!"

How nice to have company!
Sophie thought. *It will make the walk feel so much shorter.*

The group continued into town. As they passed the library, the door opened. Mrs. Reeve hurried down the steps.

"Headed to Firefly Springs?" Mrs. Reeve asked them. "May I join you? Oh, what an exciting day!"

Mrs. Reeve was coming to watch too!

And as they walked on, the group got bigger and bigger. Mr. Handy came out from the hardware store. Miss Olsen joined them as they passed the apple orchard.

Sophie's friend Owen and his mom caught up to them. "We wouldn't miss this for the world!" Owen said.

And then Mayor Squirrel met up with them at an intersection. "Well, what a sweet parade we have here— or should I say, a parade of sweets!" she said. "Escorting our bakers to the big contest? Wonderful show of support!"

Sophie could hardly believe it. So many friends were coming to root for them.

She looked at her mom, who seemed equally shocked.

"Sophie," Mrs. Mouse whispered, "how does everyone know I entered?"

Sophie hesitated. "From me, I guess," she said bashfully.

All of a sudden, Lily was looking a little flushed—and very nervous.

chapter 7

A Bellyful of
Butterflies

The parade wound its way through the forest and on to Firefly Springs. Once they got close, it was easy to find the exact spot. They just followed the sound of the crowd.

Sophie's jaw dropped. "There are so many spectators!" she cried out.

They had come out of the trees into a clearing. On one side were rows and rows of benches crowded with animals. On the other side was a large brick oven. Around the oven were six large tables set up with baking tools.

"Those must be the workstations," said Mrs. Mouse. "One for each baker."

Just then a well-dressed raccoon hurried over. "Welcome!" he said to Lily and Sophie. "My name is Stu Potts. I'm one of the judges." He eyed the baskets of baked goods. "You must be bakers, yes?"

Mrs. Mouse introduced herself.

"And this is my daughter, Sophie. She's my helper."

"Very good," Mr. Potts replied. "Each baker and helper gets a workstation. I'll show you to yours."

Lily and Sophie went with Mr. Potts. Sophie turned to wave good-bye to

help it—she peeked. A few of them were very large and fancy-looking.

A few minutes later, Sophie spotted her dad and brother. They had arrived just in time. The judges were gathered around the judging table, about to begin.

their friends, who went to find seats in the *very large* audience. Sophie was starting to feel as nervous as her mom looked.

"This will be your home base for round two," Mr. Potts said. He led them to a table. Then Mr. Potts pointed to another, much longer table nearby. "And that is the judging table for round one. You can place your baked goods there. Round one will begin shortly. Good luck to you!"

The butterflies in Sophie's stomach started doing flips. She and her mom looked at each other.

"Well, here we go!" Mrs. Mouse said, taking a deep breath. "Let's have some fun!"

They hurried over to the judging table. Sophie carefully unloaded the treats. Lily neatly arranged them on platters.

Sophie tried not to look at the other bakers' creations. But she couldn't

"Look at the size of that doughnut tower!" Sophie heard Winston cry. He pointed at the largest item in the center of the judging table.

Sophie's heart fell. Would the judges be more impressed by the look of the desserts, or the taste?

Sophie crossed her fingers. She'd have to wait and see.

— chapter 8 —

ROUND 1	ROUND 2	TOTAL

The cookie challenge

Sophie sat on the edge of her bench. The judges were posting the scores for round one.

Mr. Potts stood next to a large scoreboard. "Bakers may receive a maximum of five points per baked good," he announced. "So the highest possible score for round one is twenty points."

Then another judge started writing
the scores.

BAKER	ROUND 1	ROUND 2	TOTAL
PHIL RYE	15		
RACHEL REED	19		
MORRIS STONE	15		
LILY MOUSE	18		
MAYA BANKS	12		
EVIE TWILIGHT	20		

Sophie squeezed
her mom's hand.
Eighteen! Lily was
in the top three.
She was just two
points behind Evie
Twilight, who had
made that doughnut tower. It
was very impressive-looking. Sophie
bet it was delicious, too.

It was time for round two. "Bakers,
to your workstations!" Mr. Potts
announced.

Lily and Sophie hurried off to their
workstation. They put on the aprons

and chef hats that were hanging there.

All eyes were on Mr. Potts. The crowd was so silent you could hear a utensil drop. *Clang!* Sophie jumped. She had accidentally knocked a whisk off the counter.

"Okay. This year's baking challenge is . . . ," Mr. Potts began. He flipped the scoreboard around. On the other side, it read:

CHOCOLATE CHIP COOKIES

"Bakers, you have one hour," said Mr. Potts. "Impress us with your chocolate chip cookies. Ingredients

are stocked in your workstations.
Picking additional ingredients
from the forest *is* allowed!
The timer starts . . . now!"

Mr. Potts had a large
hourglass. He turned it
upside down. Grains of
sand started running through
the funnel.

All the other bakers sprang into action.

But Sophie and her mom first put their heads together. They needed to make a plan.

"That's it?" Sophie whispered. "Chocolate chip cookies? That seems so easy."

Mrs. Mouse twirled her whisker. "It's easy to make a tasty one," she agreed. "Everyone has a good choc-olate chip cookie recipe. The question is: How can we make ours different from the rest?"

Sophie nodded. Right. The cookie that got the judges' attention—the cookie that really stood out—would surely get the highest score.

Sophie thought about the doughnut tower. "We could make one really large cookie," she suggested. "Like a cookie cake?"

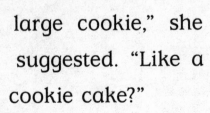

"That could work," Lily replied. "Or we could make special chips. Like cinnamon chocolate chips? Or basil chocolate chips? Maple chocolate chips?"

Maple. Sophie remembered another Maple Festival recipe she'd come up with. Maple-glazed waffles with a layer of whipped cream in between. Waffle sandwiches!

"Mom!" Sophie whispered. "What if we make cookie sandwiches? Two chocolate chip cookies with whipped cream in between?"

Lily nodded and smiled. "Ooh, that sounds good," she said. "I love it. Let's do it!"

Lily pulled out the mixing bowls. But Sophie hesitated.

"Mom, are you sure?" Sophie said.

Now she was doubting herself. Was this idea good enough to win?

If it wasn't, it would be all Sophie's fault.

"Maybe we should think about it some more?" Sophie added.

Mrs. Mouse turned to Sophie. She gently cradled Sophie's face in her hands. "We are in this together," she said. "Whatever happens. Win or lose. And your idea is the best one we have right now."

Sophie glanced over at the hourglass. Time was running away.

"So what do you say?" Lily asked.

Sophie smiled and picked up a whisk. "Let's get started," she said.

— chapter 9 —

Mint to Be

Sophie and her mom had made chocolate chip cookies together a thousand times.

Sophie assisted, handing her mom ingredients. Mrs. Mouse knew all the measurements by heart.

In a flash, the batter was done. Sophie dropped dollops of batter onto a baking sheet. Her mom slid it into the big brick oven.

Sophie whipped the cream for the filling. Her mom added a splash of vanilla.

When the cookies were done, Mrs. Mouse moved them onto a rack to cool. Sophie eyed the hourglass nervously. They couldn't put the whipped cream

between two warm
cookies. It would make
a runny mess. Sophie
just wished they would
hurry up and cool!

Finally Mrs. Mouse assembled a
cookie sandwich: two cookies and
one heaping scoop of whipped cream
in between.

"Taste test!" Sophie exclaimed. She took a bite. Mrs. Mouse took one too.

They chewed. They looked at each other.

"It's good," said Sophie. "But—"

"It needs something," Mrs. Mouse

There it was! A whiff of something that smelled promising. Sophie focused on the smell and let it lead her. She walked twenty paces. She turned and went ten more. She stopped. She opened her eyes. She looked down.

"Mint!"

It was a beautiful flowering plant. Sophie raced back to her mom with mint in hand.

Would there be enough time to use it?

~chapter 10~

And the winner is . . .

"Time's up!" Mr. Potts called out.

The last grain of sand had fallen. Sophie's mom had just placed a finishing touch on their cookie: a single perfect mint leaf.

"Please bring your finished cookie to the judging table," Mr. Potts announced.

Lined up next to one another, each

of the cookies looked so different.

Rachel Reed had made a cookie cake. "Phew," Sophie whispered to her mom. "Glad we didn't go with that idea."

Then the bakers joined the audience. They watched as the judges tasted the cookies.

One by one, they tasted. They whispered. They wrote on their clipboards. For each cookie, a judge wrote something on the back side of the scoreboard.

What were they writing? Ooh, Sophie wished she could see. There was nothing more Sophie or her

mother could do. But this was the most nervous Sophie had been all day. Waiting was so hard!

At last, the judges faced the audience.

"We have the results of round two," said Mr. Potts. "Bakers received a maximum of ten points in this round. That will be added to the

CHOCOLATE
CHIP
COOKIE

scores from round one. The baker
with the highest grand total is our
Year's Best Baker!"

With that, Mr. Potts flipped
the chalkboard around. Now the
scoreboard was showing again. The
round two scores had been filled in.

BAKER	ROUND 1	ROUND 2	TOTAL
PHIL RYE	15	8	23
RACHEL REED	19	6	25
MORRIS STONE	15	8	23
LILY MOUSE	18	10	28
MAYA BANKS	12	9	21
EVIE TWILIGHT	20	7	27

Mrs. Mouse gasped. Sophie jumped up off the bench. The crowd burst into applause. There was a cheer from the Pine Needle Grovers.

"What does it mean?" Winston cried out, confused.

Sophie lifted Winston up in celebration. "It means Mom won!" Sophie exclaimed. "MOM WON!"

Lily Mouse was called up to receive her award—a shiny medal on a blue ribbon.

As she stood up, Mrs. Mouse grabbed Sophie's hand. "You're coming too!" she said.

"Congratulations!" Mr. Potts said to them. "Your cookie was a delicious combination of soft chocolaty cookie and cool, minty cream. Refreshing, not too sweet. A wonderful balance of flavors. And very unique!"

Lily and Sophie basked in the cheers and applause. The other bakers crowded around to congratulate them. Sophie smiled up at her mom. Her mom smiled at her. That was the very best part.

At home that night, Sophie sat down at her easel. She hadn't painted all week. She had been too busy getting ready for the bake off.

Now, before she went to bed, Sophie wanted to capture the day

in a painting. She took a moment to think. What about today did she want to remember forever?

The beauty of their finished cookie?

The size of the cheering crowd?

The look on her mom's face when she won?

Then Sophie knew. It *was* a moment during the bake off. But not the big, exciting scene at the end. It was a quieter moment just between Sophie and her mom.

Sophie knew that it would always remind her of something: Her mom was on her team, no matter what.

The End

the adventures of
SOPHIE MOUSE

For excerpts, activities, and more about
these adorable tales & tails, visit
AdventuresofSophieMouse.com!